The Mystery of the Haunted House

Sycamore Street Mysteries #1

By Willow Night

Illustrated by Elizabeth Leach

Look for all the Sycamore Street Mysteries:

- *The Mystery of the Haunted House*
- *The Mystery of the Toxic Playground*
- *The Mystery of the Stolen Necklace*
- *The Mystery of the Missing Books*
- *The Mystery of the Old Town Hall*

Find out more at willownight.com

Chapter 1

Noah Walker did not like being interrupted. He had already been interrupted by the cat walking on his papers and chasing his pencil across the table.

Then Mom came through and asked about school and if he had turned in his paper. Now Noah could hear his little brother calling him. He didn't answer.

"Noah!" Noah's little brother Josh was shouting his name from the clubhouse. "Noah! Come here, it's done! I finished it!"

Noah kept doing his math homework. He had no idea what Josh was shouting about.

Josh burst into the room. He was wearing shorts and a T-shirt even though it was not that warm yet. He was excited, and his blond hair was a little sweaty from running around. The back door stood wide open and the birds were singing in the spring air.

"Noah! Come and check out my set-up in the treehouse. I have the kitchen bugged! I can hear Mom and Dad talking over the walkie-talkie!"

"Josh, it's a clubhouse. It's not in a tree so it's not a treehouse. And I am doing my homework," Noah added.

"It's Friday! You have all weekend to do that. Stop working and come check out my spy setup with the walkie-talkies." Josh pulled on Noah's arm. "Come on, I heard Mom and Dad talking about the Haunted House."

There was a house down the street from Noah and Josh that they called the Haunted House. It used to have a nice family living in it, but after they moved away it stayed empty for a long time.

No one wanted to buy the house and some of the kids on Sycamore Street said the house was haunted.

Noah didn't believe in haunted houses, but there was something funny about that empty house. He *did* want to know what Mom and

Dad were saying about it. And he wanted to see what Josh had rigged up with the walkie-talkies.

Noah closed his math book and stood up. He ran his hand through his short brown hair and stretched. He followed Josh out the back door and across their small backyard to the clubhouse next to the oak tree.

The clubhouse was high on wooden posts and had a wooden ladder. A rope with knots hung out the window.

Josh started to climb up the rope.

"Ahh!" he yelled as the rope came loose and Josh fell to the ground. The rope fell out of the window and Noah picked it up to look at it.

"Josh, are you okay? This rope isn't safe. What did you attach it to?"

Josh jumped up. "I'm fine! I'm working on a way to attach it to the window. I guess the hook I tried isn't strong enough."

Josh always thought he could climb anything, and he liked to rig up his own ropes and ladders. Mom and Dad went a little crazy trying to keep Josh off the roof. He went to climbing classes at a local gym, but it looked like he was still trying to make his own courses.

Noah and Josh hurried up the ladder and Noah looked around the clubhouse. When they were younger, they had built this house under the tree with Dad's help. They would play out here every day, even when it was raining. The roof didn't leak at all.

Now his brother Josh had all of his supplies stacked in the clubhouse. His binoculars and ropes, his flashlights and his walkie-talkies. Josh was always packing up supplies to go on "missions" and begging Noah to come along.

Noah had a lot of work to do for school. Sixth graders had much more homework than fourth graders, and Josh didn't seem to understand that. He said that Noah never played with him anymore.

Right now there was a walkie-talkie duct-taped to the wall. Josh turned the volume up on the side and Noah heard Mom's voice. The other walkie-talkie must have been set up in the kitchen.

"... who is going to buy it now? That house has been for sale for almost two years! And it looks terrible. I hope they called the police," Mom was saying.

Noah and Josh looked at each other. Some kids said they saw strange flashes at night in the windows of the Haunted House. One kid said he heard bumps and scratching sounds from inside the house when he walked his dog by there.

What could have happened to the house that the police had to be called? Had someone broken in? Noah hoped there wasn't a fire.

Dad talked next.

"I asked the real estate agent who would clean it up and she said she would try to get in touch with the owners. But she didn't know when they would answer her emails."

Noah listened closely, wondering what needed to be cleaned up. The Haunted House looked sad and spooky, but it wasn't dirty or messy.

"Did they find anything else at the house besides the writing on the front?" Mom asked. "No. There were no broken windows or graffiti on the sides or the back," answered Dad.

"Do you think it was kids who did it?" wondered Mom.

"I don't see how any kids could have gotten up high enough to paint above the upstairs windows without getting inside the house. Even an adult would have a hard time reaching that spot with a ladder. The house is locked and protected with a security system," said Dad.

"So there is writing on the house and we don't know how anyone could do it without getting inside the house, which is locked and guarded with an alarm. What did the writing say anyway?" asked Mom.

"Just one word," answered Dad. "Beware."

Chapter 2

"Whoa. Let's go check it out," Josh said to Noah.

Noah took a deep breath and thought about his math. "What about my homework? I have a lot to do this weekend."

"Noah! You are always doing homework. You never have time to go on missions with me anymore. A crime at the Haunted House! We need to see this."

"Painting on someone's house isn't a felony, Josh. But I guess I have time to ride down there if it's quick."

Noah and Josh grabbed their bikes and helmets from the garage.

"Wait! I need my supplies." Josh climbed back up the ladder and came back down with a backpack. "Now I'm ready."

"What do you have in there?" Noah asked.

"Just my flashlight and binoculars and some supplies in case we need them. It's good to be prepared. And granola bars, don't worry."

Since it was still afternoon Noah didn't see why they would need a flashlight, but he didn't argue with the snacks.

When the brothers saw the Haunted House they could read the word "Beware" right away. It was painted in red paint up at the top just under the roof.

Noah and Josh looked up, wondering how someone could have painted on the house all the way up there.

"Maybe they had a super-tall ladder, like for working on the roof," Noah suggested.

"But wouldn't someone see a ladder that big? It was probably the ghosts," Josh added, half joking.

Just then the front door opened, and a tall woman walked out, followed by a man who frowned and looked mad.

Josh and Noah rolled their bikes next to a little library box across the street. The brothers pretended to look at the books inside while they listened to what the woman and the man said.

"This house costs way too much!" The grumpy man almost shouted. "And now it's worth even less money. The owner should take my offer. He is lucky that I even want to buy a haunted house!"

The woman was the real estate agent for the house. She smiled and told the man that she would let the owners know that he still wanted to buy the house.

"I've been trying to buy this house all year! Why won't they sell it to me?" The man was yelling at the woman. "You're not doing your job! Your job is to sell this house—to me!"

The woman sighed, and Josh and Noah hoped the man would stop shouting and go away. The man climbed into his car and slammed the door, driving away too fast for a road where kids played.

Noah and Josh crossed the street. "I'm sorry about the house," Josh said to the woman as she pushed the buttons for the alarm and locked the door.

"It's okay." The woman didn't look upset as she put the keys away in her purse. "Nothing you kids need to worry about."

"What's going to happen with the graffiti?" Noah asked.

The woman shrugged. "We'll get it cleaned up. You boys should go off and play somewhere else now." She smiled politely and waved as she got in her car and drove off.

"Why was that man so mad about the house?" Josh asked Noah.

"I guess he wants to buy it, but the owners won't agree. Maybe the owners want a lot of money for it. I wonder if he would paint on the house to make the owner want to get rid of it and sell it? It's more likely than a ghost!"

Noah turned to see what Josh thought about his idea, but Josh was peering around the corner of the house.

"Noah! There's someone sneaking in the bushes in the backyard," Josh said quietly.

Noah came over to his brother and peeked around the corner of the house. There was a shadow behind a big bush that could be a person wearing dark clothes and crouching down.

"Maybe it's the ghost!" Josh said. "Let's go see!"

Noah was interested. "Hang on. Let's lock up our bikes and sneak around the other side."

"Good idea!" Josh whispered. "Act like we're leaving now."

Noah said in a loud voice, "Come on, Josh, time to go home now." They crossed back to the little library and chained their bikes and helmets to the post. Then they walked quietly to the other corner of the house and snuck through the bushes on that side.

Noah heard the sound of something moving through branches up ahead. Was it a cat or a dog? The branches were thick, but he thought he could see a dark shape that looked too short to be a grownup.

Just then Josh stepped on a stick and a loud crack rang out. The dark shape froze and then whoever it was sprinted across the backyard and jumped over the low fence. All they could see from the back was dark clothes and dark curly hair in a ponytail.

"Let's get out of here," said Noah.

"No, let's go see who it is!" Josh cried as he ran towards the fence and leaped into the next yard.

Chapter 3

Noah ran after his brother and caught up with him.

"Where did they go?" he panted.

"The kid? Ran between those houses," Josh called as he raced off. Josh was fast. He was probably the fastest fourth grader in the school and Noah had to run hard to keep up with him. He couldn't see anyone, but he could hear the sound of pounding footsteps up ahead.

The brothers ran down an alley and swung around to the right, chasing the sound of the footsteps. The kid dashed across the street and between two houses into another backyard.

"We shouldn't be running through all these yards," Noah panted as they finally stopped in the backyard of a yellow and white house. He wondered if this kid was the one who had painted *Beware* on the house. Maybe this was the "ghost" that was causing the flashing lights and bumps and noises from inside the Haunted House.

"Hang on, where did they go?" Josh looked all around and listened. They couldn't hear footsteps anymore. But they saw movement on the side of the house as a door opened and a dark figure stepped inside.

"Come on Josh, to the shadow of that tree-" Noah pulled Josh over to the side of the yard. They could see a deck, empty and getting dark as the sun went down. Behind the deck a light flipped on in the kitchen of the house.

A woman walked into the kitchen carrying a baby. She placed the baby in a highchair and gave her a banana. Then a girl walked into the room. The girl was wearing dark clothes and had a big ponytail of curly dark hair.

"That's the kid we followed!" Josh gasped. The girl paused and looked out the window and down at her watch.

"Wait, can she see us?" Josh asked Noah.

"No, it's getting dark," Noah answered. "I know that girl, she's a new sixth grader. I think her name is Olivia." Olivia was helping her mom make dinner while her little sister made a big mess with the banana.

"Do you think she painted on the house? She was spying on it!" Josh wondered.

"So were we," replied Noah. "But it is funny that she ran away like that. If she wasn't doing anything wrong, why did she run away?"

In the kitchen Olivia's mom was looking for something in the fridge.

While Noah and Josh stood in the shadow of the tree, Olivia turned to the window and waved a little wave so her mom wouldn't see. She held up one finger, silently mouthing the words, "one minute." She turned and said something to her mom and started pulling a bag of garbage out of the bin.

"She *can* see us! Did you see that?" Josh demanded.

Noah thought hard. "It's too dark for her to be able to see us. She must know we followed her. Maybe she just thinks we *might* be back here. I don't understand. Let's wait a minute and see."

Inside Olivia had the bag of garbage and checked her watch again and glanced out the window. It seemed like she was looking right into the corner where Noah and Josh were hidden. A moment later she was outside bringing the garbage to a big bin on the side of the house.

Then, after a peek through the window at her mother and little sister, she ducked and ran to the corner under the tree.

"Why were you spying on the Haunted House?" she demanded.

"Hey, you were spying first. And you ran away from us. Also, how did you know we were back here?" Josh answered back.

Olivia stared at Josh and adjusted her ponytail. Then she looked at Noah. "You're Noah," she said.

Noah nodded. "This is my little brother Josh. He's in fourth grade. You're Olivia, right? And you're new?"

Olivia nodded and stared at Josh. "Can fourth graders keep secrets?" she asked him, narrowing her eyes.

Josh gulped and answered, "Yes."

Olivia thought a moment and made up her mind. She said, "I knew you were back here because I have my backyard wired." She pointed to a branch they couldn't reach, where they could see the outline of wires. She held up her wrist with a smart watch. "Speech to text program. I can read what anyone is saying back here."

"Whoa," Josh gasped. "That is so cool."

"Look," Noah said. "It's dark and I have to take him home. Do you have any information about the Haunted House? Do you know what's going on there?"

"Yeah, I've got some dirt on it," Olivia answered. "But I gotta go, too. Do you have text or email?"

Noah sighed. "No." He got this a lot. "My parents ..." he trailed off. His parents didn't believe in kids having phones.

Olivia nodded. "I'm free tomorrow afternoon. We can share information."

"Okay, we live at 314 Sycamore Street," Josh said. "Are you going to bring your tech?"

Olivia smiled. "Maybe. Let me know if you see anything on the way home." She glanced at the window where her mom was cooking in the kitchen and her little sister was starting to throw banana on the floor. "See ya."

"Bye," Noah muttered. "Come on, Josh." He tugged on his little brother, who was straining to see the wires in the branches.

Noah and Josh walked out to the road and headed back to Sycamore Street. They had to stop and pick up their bikes from the little library across from the Haunted House. As Noah did the combination on the bike lock, Josh grabbed his arm.

"Noah, look!" Josh whispered.

Noah turned around slowly. Upstairs in the Haunted House the blinds were drawn. But between the cracks Noah could see flashes of light. A bunch of flashes in a row, then a pause, then a bunch more. The flashes were bright, brighter than regular house lights. All of a sudden, the flashing stopped, and the windows were dark once more.

Chapter 4

Noah and Josh waited in silence, staring up towards the windows. But the Haunted House stayed dark. Finally, they gave up and rode their bikes home for dinner.

The next morning was Saturday. Noah was planning to sleep in, but his family was up early, making noise and pancakes. Even the cat jumped up on his bed and tried to nuzzle his face through the covers.

Noah gave up and got up. He headed downstairs and found Josh and his parents sitting at the table in the kitchen, eating pancakes.

"Grab a plate, there's some for you," Mom greeted him. Noah liked his pancakes with butter and maple syrup.

"Were you guys out biking in the neighborhood last night?" Dad asked.

"Yeah. We saw the graffiti on the Haunted House," Noah told him.

Josh jumped in, "And we saw this real estate agent and a mad guy who was shouting and ..." Josh trailed off as Noah caught his eye. Noah shook his head a little. He didn't think his parents would want them to get involved.

"It's probably better if you stay away from there," Mom said. "They are going to be looking for whoever painted on the house, and I don't want you to get in trouble."

"We'll be careful," Noah promised.

After breakfast Noah put his shoes on. "Come on," he said to Josh.

"Where are we going?" asked Josh.

"You'll see," Noah said.

"Remember, leave that house alone," Mom called as they left out the back door.

Josh followed close behind as Noah went around the clubhouse and behind the garage and down the alley.

"This is cool. What's down here?" Josh wondered, looking around.

Noah told him to wait a minute as they came to another garage halfway down the block. From inside the garage they could hear loud electric guitar and drums and the whine of a saw. Josh looked nervous, but Noah pounded on the door.

The door was yanked open by a short bald man wearing goggles and covered in sawdust. When he saw the brothers, he moved aside and yelled over the music, "Hi Noah! Who's this?"

Noah pulled Josh inside the garage where the music was even louder. Josh held back a little bit, but Noah bent down to shout. "It's okay. This is Bill. He builds things."

"Bill the builder?" Josh shouted back.

"Don't call him that!" Noah warned.

But Bill was laughing. "It's okay."

"This is my brother Josh." Noah said in a loud voice. "He likes to build things too."

"What do you build?" Bill called as he went to turn the music down. A little bit.

Josh looked at the tools and tables all over the garage. "Right now I'm working on a way to hook a rope to a window. So I can climb down the side of our treehouse. So far, the hooks fall out or they are too heavy. I want to carry it around in my backpack." He looked behind him and seemed to miss his supplies.

Bill had a gleam in his eye. "Hmm, interesting." He started poking around in a pile of scrap metal on the side of the room.

"Hey Bill, do you know anything about a ghost in the house for sale down the block?" Noah called.

Bill turned back and gazed at the brothers. "A ghost? Come on." He shook his head as he picked up part of a broken metal fence. "Hmm."

"We saw something there last night. Flashing lights," Noah told him.

"You saw that too?" Bill seemed distracted. He pulled out a helmet with a face mask that fit on his whole head. Josh looked nervously over to Noah.

"That's a mask for welding. It's okay. Bill, what do you think those lights are? A ghost?" Noah asked.

"No such thing as ghosts." Bill fitted the helmet on his head. "I saw those lights the other night driving home. A bunch of flashes in a row, right? Real bright?"

"Yeah," Josh nodded. "How could anyone get inside a house with the lock and the alarm on?"

"Aw, alarms, there's ways around that," Bill scoffed. "You just need some basic electric skills, run a few wires. Get around that in no time."

Noah and Josh looked at each other. Noah thought about Olivia and how she said she had her backyard wired. But Olivia had been home at her house when they saw the lights.

"Why would someone break into a house to flash the lights?" Noah asked, feeling confused.

"Maybe they want people to think there's a ghost in there. Maybe they're taking pictures of something. I don't know. What do you think?" Bill put the broken piece of fence on a table and pulled out some thick cables and clamps.

He cracked a window at the back of the garage and pulled on a jacket that was hanging on the wall.

"You boys want to see some welding? Watch this. But don't look directly at the light," Bill said sternly.

"Why not?" asked Josh.

"Look, it's not good for your eyes. It's 240 volts of electricity." Bill looked over at Noah. "Maybe you two should head home," he told them as he pulled on big gloves. "I'm gonna make something I think will work for your treehouse rope, Josh. I'll bring it by later."

"Come on, Josh," Noah pulled his brother out the door.

"But I wanted to see him do it! Why can't we look at it?" Josh begged.

"We will another time. But you can't be in Bill's garage unless you are going to listen to him and not argue."

The music was turned back up and now they heard hissing and popping noises from the garage. The boys looked at each other and headed home.

Chapter 5

After lunch Josh ran out to the clubhouse and Noah grabbed a book to read on the couch. This was not turning out to be a quiet weekend, and he still had most of his homework to do.

The cat walked over to him. She was waiting for him to move so she could take his warmed-up spot.

"Forget about it," Noah told her, and pulled a blanket over his legs as he flipped through the novel they were reading for Language Arts.

"Noah!" Josh called.

Noah sighed and leaned back to peer out the window. He jumped in his seat, startled. Josh was standing right outside the window. Next to him was Olivia. She smiled and waved.

They turned and ran across the backyard to the clubhouse. Noah put his book down and followed. "You can have the spot, I guess," he told the cat.

Outside Noah was holding the knotted rope and pointing to the window. "And this guy Bill is going to weld me a hook or something to attach it!" he was saying.

"Cool." Olivia was wearing jeans and a T-shirt. Her curly hair was in a ponytail and she had a messenger bag slung over her shoulder. "Is there someplace I can put my bike?"

"Anywhere is fine," Noah answered. They all stood around for a minute looking at the clubhouse and around the yard. Noah wasn't sure what they were going to do now.

"Come on, let's start the meeting!" Josh climbed up the ladder, pulling the rope after him, and disappeared through the door of the clubhouse.

Noah glanced at Olivia, who shrugged and followed. So Noah climbed up after Olivia and ducked through the door.

Josh had dragged a couple of beanbag chairs up. Maybe with his rope. Noah sat down while Olivia looked at Josh's supplies.

"Wow," she said, "you're ready for anything, aren't you?"

There were several sets of binoculars that Josh had hanging on the wall. There were a couple lengths of cord and rope that he had collected from somewhere. In a crate were cans of seltzer water and granola bars next to a small pile of flashlights and a sleeping bag.

Josh also had a table piled with compasses, a magnifying glass, a small microscope, a first aid kit, batteries, Swiss army knives, duct tape, and for some reason, socks.

"Nice socks," Olivia laughed, but she also looked impressed.

"I'm a prepper," Josh told her. "Like, a person who prepares for stuff." He pulled out a couple of old backpacks and tossed them on the floor. "In case you guys need anything. Okay, let the meeting begin!"

Josh sat down on a second beanbag chair and Olivia took the third.

"On our way home last night we saw lights in the Haunted House," Noah started.

"What did they look like?" Olivia asked.

"A bunch of bright flashes, then a pause, then more flashes. Then it all went dark and nothing else."

"I gotta get a camera up over there," Olivia said. "I usually use the internet, so I've been saving for a camera that works without Wi-Fi. I was scouting out a spot to put it yesterday."

"That's what you were doing!" Josh said. "Are you trying to solve the mystery of the Haunted House?"

"Well, yeah. I don't believe in ghosts."

"How do you buy your own security cameras?" Noah asked.

"I babysit a lot," Olivia told him. "So much. We just moved here, and I don't have any friends yet, anyway." The boys thought about that. They didn't know you could make that much money babysitting.

Olivia pulled a tablet from her bag and opened a maps app. She zoomed in on a satellite image of the neighborhood until it showed the Haunted House and yard and the streets around it.

They looked at the trees and bushes in the yard and talked about where a wireless security camera could go. Olivia told them how she could point a camera at the back of the house and watch the footage on her phone or laptop. "Hello! Anyone up there?" called a man's voice from below. Josh stuck his head out of the clubhouse window.

"Hi Bill!" He looked over at Noah. Noah came over to the window and looked down. Bill was standing there with a paper grocery bag in his hand.

"Special delivery," said Bill. "I made this for your little brother there."

Josh grinned, grabbed his rope and ran to the door calling, "Wow! Thank you! Here I come!" Josh climbed down, and Bill pulled a metal hook out of the bag and they started talking about it.

Noah smiled. Josh was so excited. He was glad that Bill had made the hook for Josh.

"Who's that?" Olivia asked.

"Bill, from the garage down the alley," Noah answered. "Well, he works in the garage. He must live in the house."

Olivia swiped on her tablet Noah showed her which garage was Bill's. It wasn't hard to see because of the scrap lumber and funny metal sculptures he had piled in his yard.

"He's a good guy," Noah said. "He can make all kinds of stuff. And he doesn't mind kids popping in to say hi."

"Good to know ..." Olivia started to say. Then they both turned as they heard Josh saying "Bill, we're going to find out what's going on with the Haunted House tonight."

Olivia and Noah ran to the clubhouse window in time to hear Bill say, "And just how are you going to do that, buddy?"

Chapter 6

"Josh!" Noah called in a low warning voice. Bill looked up.

"What are y'all up to, Noah?" he asked.

"We're just curious, that's all," Olivia said in a friendly voice. "We're going to keep our eyes and ears open for any developments."

Bill looked a little suspicious, but he nodded.

"Well, kids, enjoy that climbing hook. I'm out," he said and waved as he headed back up the alley.

"Thanks again!" Noah called.

Josh yelled, "Thank you, Bill!"

Noah looked down at Josh. He knew Josh wasn't trying to get them in trouble, but he wasn't sure Josh was good at this undercover stuff. "Come back up here a minute," he said to his brother.

Josh made a nervous face and slowly climbed up the ladder.

Noah was glad when Olivia started talking first.

"Josh, if we're going to work together on this, we have to be careful what we say to people." She said it nicely. "Putting up a camera on private property is, well, against the law. I could get into trouble."

Josh looked grumpy. "I can keep a secret. Besides, it was my idea to check out the house in the first place." He looked over at Noah.

"Okay, well, no one has to help if they don't want to. Are we all in?"

"I'm in," said Noah.

"Me too," said Josh.

"Me too," said Olivia. "Okay, I'll plant the camera tonight and then I'll call you to touch base. You do have a home phone, right?"

"Yes, of course," Noah replied, and he gave her the number.

"Wait, you're going to hook up the camera without us?" asked Josh. "I want to go, too."

Olivia thought for a few seconds and then shook her head. "The more kids, the more chance we'll be seen. Don't worry, if I see something good on the feed, we can all check it out. I'll call you," she told him.

Josh agreed, and Olivia packed her bag and got up to go.

"I have a quick babysitting job and then as soon as it's dark I'll stop at the house. I'll call you when it's done."

"Okay, talk to you later," Noah said as Olivia climbed down the ladder and put on her bike helmet.

Noah also got ready to leave. At least he could finally try to get some homework done. Josh looked a little upset, but Noah knew he was just wishing he could go on the mission to plant the camera.

The boys had dinner with Mom and Dad and by the end of dinner it was getting dark.

"Do you want to play a game?" Mom asked while they cleaned up. Noah looked around.

Josh had already gone back to the clubhouse. "Um ... I think not tonight Mom. Sorry. Josh is doing a project and I need to finish my math."

"Okay." Their mom looked surprised. The boys rarely turned down an offer to play cards or a board game.

Noah settled down to work on his math homework, but he kept one ear open for the phone. He looked out the window now and then and wondered what was going on with Olivia. Had she gotten the camera up at the Haunted House yet?

An hour went by with no word from Olivia. Then the phone rang. Dad walked over but Noah called, "I got it!" and ran to answer first.

"Hello? Hey Olivia, it's me, Noah," he said.

"Oookay," Dad said, with a look. Noah didn't get a lot of phone calls.

"Noah," said Olivia. "It's done. I put the camera in the branches of the maple tree in the side yard. It points straight at the back door."

"Wow. Good work," Noah said quietly as he walked out of the kitchen and into the empty dining room. "See anything good yet?"

"I'm just setting the program up. I don't have the feed yet. Wait—here it is," Olivia answered. "Whoa, Noah, something's going on. There are people in the backyard."

"Who?" Noah asked.

"I can't tell. They're wearing dark clothes and the lights are off. Shoot. I should have put some kind of infrared lens on the camera. There was a light on in the backyard, but it looks like someone turned it off."

"Okay," Noah said, "I'll find Josh. Should we ride past the house and see if we can turn the light on in the back?" Noah went out the back door and crossed the yard calling, "Josh," softly.

"Um, not sure about that," said Olivia. "What if the people see you? Hey, they've got some kind of equipment. They're making a pile by the back door."

"Okay, we'll ride to your house and make a plan," he suggested.

"That works. Wow, let me get this set up to record," Olivia said to herself.

"Okay, Josh should be right here. Josh? Josh?" There was no answer from the clubhouse. Noah looked all around the yard. The house was dark except for his parents, who were still in the kitchen laughing and cleaning up. Josh wasn't in the yard.

"Hang on," Noah said to Olivia.

He climbed up the ladder and poked his head into the clubhouse. No Josh. Noah looked over to the corner by the garage where they had dropped their bikes.

"Um, Olivia," Noah said into the phone, "I don't see Josh. Or his backpack. Or his bike."

Chapter 7

Noah was worried and a little bit scared. It was dark, and Josh had left. Why had he gone off by himself?

Olivia sighed, "Do you think he went over to the house?"

"Yeah. I guess we'd better go find him. He's not supposed to be riding his bike by himself when it's dark," Noah said.

"Also, there are still people at the house! And I can't tell what they are doing. Okay. Let's meet at the little library in ten minutes," Olivia suggested.

"Okay," Noah agreed.

"Are you going to tell your parents?" Olivia asked.

"I'll let them know I'm going to get him."

* * *

Noah told his parents that Josh was probably over at their new friend's house and that he was going to go get him.

"Okay, be careful on your bike. Bring your light," Dad told him.

Noah got ready and turned on the light for his bike. He rode down to the Haunted House and stopped at the little library across the street.

Josh was definitely here. His bike was locked to the post. Noah locked up his bike and opened the tiny door to look at the books inside. He tried to act like he was just looking for a good book to read.

Olivia pulled up and locked her bike with the others. They stood side by side, pulling out books and flipping through them.

"Have you seen him?" Olivia asked in a low voice.

"No. But his bike is here. What's going on in the back?" Noah asked.

Olivia pulled out her phone and opened an app that showed mostly darkness.

"It's really hard to see with the outdoor light turned off. But I've got some audio. Hold on, let me change it to text." She swiped, and words appeared on the screen.

Hey, that's everything.
Can you lock up and come up?
Yeah what's the code again?
5559 and lock the door too.
Got it. I'll be right up.

Olivia smiled. "Got the alarm code. But where's your brother? I should put a tracker on him."

Noah shrugged and looked all around. Josh's bike and helmet were here. Maybe Josh had gone around to the backyard.

They walked around the corner and silently slipped up the alley toward the backyard of the Haunted House.

Olivia put her hand on Noah's arm to stop him. He looked up and they both stared at the windows of the Haunted House.

Even with the blinds closed, they could see flashing lights. Now they knew it wasn't a ghost. Someone was in there, someone who knew the code to the alarm. But where was Josh?

They reached the backyard and looked in all the bushes, sticking to the shadows as much as they could. Olivia showed Noah the camera and he waved to it. But he didn't see Josh anywhere.

In a low voice he called, "Josh! Are you here?"

There was no answer. Noah and Olivia looked at each other, deep in thought.

"Do you think he would go in the house?" Olivia asked.

"Josh? Yeah, if he had the chance," Noah said.

"We have to go in and find him," Olivia said, pulling a camera out of her bag. "And if there's anything funny going on in there, I'll take pictures."

Noah took a deep breath and agreed. Josh might be stuck in that house. He couldn't let his little brother down.

They snuck over to the back door, glad that the lights were still turned off. Olivia swung open the little panel on the house alarm and typed in 5559. There was a beep and the light flashed from red to green. Both kids held their breath and waited, wondering if anyone inside the house would notice. But there was no sound from inside.

They tried the doorknob, but it was locked. Noah slipped quietly to the window, gently lifting the screen off and pulling up on the window. It opened.

Breathing a sigh of relief, Olivia and Noah climbed through the large kitchen window as quietly as they could. Thank goodness no one remembered to lock the windows of this house!

The kitchen was dark, but they could hear low voices and footsteps upstairs above their heads. Noah froze and listened, but the footsteps were not coming closer. It sounded like a man and a woman walking around and talking in the room above them.

Olivia tiptoed into the hall and whispered, "Josh." There was no answer. She looked back at Noah. Noah felt like his heart was beating so hard the people upstairs would hear it.

He followed Olivia into the hall, and they went into a dark room just as a door opened upstairs and the footsteps got louder. The people were coming down the stairs!

Noah waited with Olivia in the shadows of the empty room, hoping no one would come in. They heard voices coming down the hallway and footsteps going into the kitchen.

Noah looked at Olivia and pointed up at the ceiling to see if she thought they should go upstairs. Olivia pulled her camera out and nodded grimly.

While the man and the woman banged around in the kitchen the two kids stepped as quietly as they could up the stairs. At the top of the stairs, one room was open with the lights on. Inside they could see big stands with lights set up and other equipment.

Noah and Olivia were about to go into the room when Noah heard someone whisper and a dark shape moved out of the doorway to their right.

Chapter 8

Olivia jumped back and gasped.

"Noah?" came a whisper out of the dark. The shape moved towards them. It was Josh, wearing all black clothes with his backpack, looking scared but determined.

"Oh, thank goodness," Olivia whispered as Noah pulled Josh into a quick hug and squeezed him.

"Ow!" said Josh quietly, pushing his big brother off.

Noah shook his head. "Josh! We were so worried!"

"Come on," Josh pulled them towards the room with the lights on. "You have to see this."

They entered the room quietly, listening for any sound of the adults returning. All around were bright lights on stands, and a printer hummed in the corner next to some other machine.

There were laptops, cameras and different kinds of paper on a table. Olivia pulled out her camera and started taking pictures of everything in the room.

The kids walked over to the table, looking at the stuff piled on it. Noah picked up a small navy booklet with "Passport" written on the cover. He opened it and held it up to show Olivia the inside.

There was a picture inside of the lady real estate agent! Noah checked several more booklets and silently pointed to the names. Each passport had the same picture but a different name. Olivia took a picture of each one.

"I don't understand," Josh whispered. "What is all this?"

"It looks like they're making fake documents," Noah answered.

"The lights must be the flash going off for the pictures," Olivia added as she walked over to look at a stand of lights with a black umbrella attached to it. She took pictures of the lights and the other equipment.

Suddenly she froze. They heard voices from the kitchen below.

"Hello?" someone called. "Did you hear that? Hello, is someone there?"

The three kids stood frozen until they heard a door slam.

Noah's heart started pounding again. He was scared. Olivia had stopped taking pictures. They all looked wildly around for a place to hide.

"Come on," Josh whispered and pulled open a door. It led into another empty room, and Noah realized it was the room Josh had been hiding in when they came upstairs. Olivia pulled the door shut with a soft click and they waited in the dark.

Trying to breathe as quietly as possible, Noah, Olivia and Josh listened to the footsteps coming up the stairs.

"Is someone there?" the woman called up from the first floor. Noah thought it was the real estate agent they had seen showing the house.

"No one in here," the man answered.

"Do you want to check the rest of the rooms just to make sure?" she called up.

Josh gasped quietly. Noah pulled him back from the door and scanned the room for options. The only other door led out into the hallway. Besides the doors there were two windows.

Remembering the unlocked window downstairs, Noah tiptoed over to the window and tried the sash. Olivia followed and they both pulled up on the window. It slid open. Olivia pushed hard on the screen and it fell down into the backyard with a clatter.

"What was that?" they heard the man say. "Did you hear that?"

Olivia looked out the window and whispered, "Too far to jump."

They heard footsteps coming down the hall.

Josh quickly pulled off his backpack and zipped it open, pulling out a length of rope and the metal hook Bill had made. They hooked it onto the windowsill and gazed down. It still looked far down, and the rope wasn't that thick.

Josh climbed up onto the window ledge and said, "It's just like the treehouse, come on." He climbed down quickly and jumped lightly onto the ground below.

Noah nodded to Olivia and she went next. He was sure the man was going to walk into the room any second. Olivia had some more trouble, but she finally made it to the ground. Noah started to climb out the window.

"Hey!" came a shout as the man finally checked the room they were in. "What are you doing?"

Noah climbed as fast as he could until he was halfway down and jumped the rest of the way. Josh tugged on the rope, but the hook was stuck at the top. They all jumped back as the man stuck his head out the window.

"Hey! Get back here!" he shouted.

"My rope!" hissed Josh.

"Gotta leave it!" Olivia told him as she dragged him back into the shadows with Noah close behind, and they took off into the night.

Chapter 9

Olivia led the way, running through the backyards away from the house.

"Olivia, our bikes!" Noah called as they ran down an alley and across a quiet street.

"We'll get them tomorrow!" Olivia yelled back. "Follow me!"

They ran as fast as they could until they all stopped, panting, in Olivia's backyard.

"Take a second," she gasped, breathing hard.

They caught their breath. Then they looked around smiling.

"We did it!" Noah said. "That was crazy, I can't believe we climbed out of the window." He put his arm around Josh. "You crazy kid!"

"Out the window," Josh sang and did a dance. "We went out the window."

Olivia laughed and asked if they wanted to come inside. They followed her into the kitchen where her mom was eating, and her little sister Emily was working her way through Cheerios in her highchair.

"Olivia!" said her mom. "I tried to text you! Sorry honey, we were hungry, and we couldn't wait any longer."

"I'm sorry Mom, I got caught up in a...project. This is Noah and Josh." She grinned at them as they both said hello to Olivia's mom and baby Emily. Emily threw some Cheerios on the floor.

"Do you want something to eat, boys? I just made mac and cheese. And we have Cheerios of course."

"Sure, if that's okay. Thanks!" said Noah and they all got plates which they piled high with macaroni and cheese for a second dinner.

"I should call my parents," Noah said after the three kids finished most of the food. They left a little bit to be polite.

Olivia pulled out her phone and handed it to Noah and he stepped out of the kitchen to call his mom. "Yeah, I'm with Josh, we're at a friend's house. Can you pick us up here in…" Noah looked over at Olivia as she mouthed the words *one hour* "…in an hour?" he finished.

Mom agreed and they all helped clear the plates.

"Mom, I want to show them something in my room, okay? We will be done in an hour," Olivia said.

"Okay!" her mom answered. "You don't want to miss Family Movie Night!"

"What's Family Movie Night?" Josh asked

Olivia shrugged.

"Probably *Frozen* again. Emily's favorite." Josh shook his head while Noah laughed. "Better you than me," he told Olivia.

"It's not that bad," she smiled. "You should see Emily dance to *Let It Go*."

* * *

Olivia had an alarm pad hooked up to the door of her room. Josh stared as she punched in a code and they heard a loud beep and a click.

Inside Olivia's room was a bed and a dresser and a collection of computer monitors, microphones, cameras and cords. She went straight to her desk and flicked on a monitor.

She opened a window on the screen that showed the back of a house with lights on inside.

"That's the Haunted House!" Josh gasped.

"Yes, this is the camera I got set up this evening." Olivia said. "See? You didn't need to go in there, we can see what's going on."

The upstairs window had been closed and there was no sign of Josh's rope. Through the windows they could see people moving around in the room where the equipment had been.

Suddenly in the camera feed the back door opened and the man walked out carrying a large, heavy-looking duffel bag. He carried it across the yard and put in the trunk of a van parked by the side of the house.

"They're getting away! They're getting away with all their stuff!" Josh exclaimed.

"Nope," said Olivia as she pulled her camera out of her messenger bag and plugged it into a laptop. "Not when we email these photos to the police!"

"Nice," Noah said. "Let's do it. Is there a way to do it anonymously? So they don't know it's us?"

"Yeah, I had to do that for babysitting once," Olivia said. "One of the parents was breaking the law." She set up the laptop to upload the photos from her camera.

They sat while the photos were loading onto the laptop.

"So, it was illegal?" Josh asked. "What they were doing in that house?"

"We think so," Olivia answered. "It looks like they were taking pictures to make fake IDs and passports. That's definitely against the law."

"Maybe that's why the house was for sale for so long," Noah wondered. "Maybe the real estate agent was using it the whole time as a workshop or whatever."

"I bet she was the one who painted Beware," Olivia pointed out.

"And she wouldn't sell it to the guy who wanted to buy it!" burst out Josh. "We did it!

We solved the mystery of the Haunted House!" He grinned as Noah and Olivia rolled their eyes. "It's okay, I know there's no such thing as ghosts."

"There," Olivia said as she unplugged the camera and the pictures opened on the screen. She found a website to send anonymous tips to the police.

She typed out a message with the info they had. Noah remembered the name of the real estate agent. And she attached the pictures of the equipment and the fake IDs.

At the bottom she typed a 10-digit number. "That's my phone number. They don't need our names, but they can send us updates. See?"

she asked as her phone dinged. On the screen was the message:

Thank you for using the Citizen Crime Reporting Service

We will contact this number when there is an update on your complaint

Your reference number is F4927549303

"Boys!" they heard Olivia's mom call upstairs. "Your dad is here to pick you up!"

They looked at Olivia and she put out her fist for a fist bump.

"Nice doing business with you. Sorry about your rope, Josh."

"Yeah, thanks for your help," Noah said. "Stop by tomorrow when you pick up your bike if you want.

"It's a plan."

Chapter 10

In the morning Noah tried once again to sleep in but Josh came into his room early. They talked about the house and the fake passports. They talked about climbing out the window and all the tech Olivia had.

Noah was glad that he was in his bed, where it was warm, and that Josh was home safe.

"You shouldn't have run off like that without telling me where you were going," he said to Josh quietly. "What happened?"

Josh nodded. "Yeah, it was a bad idea. When I got there, I locked up my bike and watched the front for a few minutes. A van pulled up on the side of the house and a man and a woman got out.

"I walked around the corner and I saw the man and woman go into the back door of the house. I thought maybe they wanted to buy the house. I snuck into the backyard to hide.

"Then they came out again and started unloading stuff from the van. They took some of it inside and I saw a light switch on upstairs. The back door was wide open, so I thought maybe I could just take a peek inside." He looked over at Noah.

Noah shook his head. "Kinda dumb. But pretty brave for a fourth grader."

Josh told Noah how he had been looking around when the adults had come back and he hid, sneaking upstairs while they went back to the van to unload more equipment.

Then he had been stuck upstairs, hiding, while they worked. He didn't know how he was going to get out because he heard them talking about setting the alarm.

"So, what did you do?" Noah asked him.

"I sat down and ate a granola bar. And drank seltzer water."

Noah stared at his little brother. "You snuck into the Haunted House, hid in the dark, had no idea how you were going to get out, and you sat around eating a granola bar?"

"I was hungry," Josh shrugged. They laughed.

* * *

After breakfast the two brothers walked down to where the bikes had been locked to the little library all night. The Haunted House looked quiet and empty in the morning light.

Olivia's bike was still there so Josh rode while Noah walked two bikes and they headed to her house, hoping she was awake.

When they got there, they walked around to the front of the house for the first time. There was a car in the driveway and a stroller, and some baby push toys piled in the front walk.

Noah rang the doorbell.

Olivia answered the door.

"We brought your bike back." Josh told her.

"Oh, thank you!" she said. "Look at the message I got this morning." She held up her wrist and they bent over the tiny screen on her watch.

This is in reference to
Citizen Crime Report: F4927549303
A warrant(s) has been issued in this case
Thank you for using the Citizen Crime
Reporting Service

"What's a warrant?" Josh asked.

"It's a paper or document from a judge that lets the police arrest someone," Olivia told him.

"The police can't just do that?" Josh asked.

Noah answered this time.

"Not if they don't see someone committing a crime. They can't just arrest you because someone said you broke the law. They have to have evidence and they show it to a judge. The judge issues a warrant if it looks like there's enough evidence that someone broke the law. Or it can be a warrant to search someplace. I wonder if they are going to search the Haunted House!"

"You have to stop calling it that." Olivia pulled her tablet out of her messenger bag, which she seemed to have with her at all times. She opened a tab and it showed the live feed from the camera she had set up behind the house.

The backyard was quiet. They didn't see anyone in the video.

"Want to ride by there just in case?" Olivia asked, grinning.

They hopped on their bikes and rode back towards Josh and Noah's house.

In front of the Haunted House there was a police car parked with a police officer sitting in it. Noah looked over at Olivia as they turned down Sycamore Street towards the Walker home. Something was happening.

Back at Noah's house they all went around to the clubhouse. When Olivia heard that Noah had a laptop for school, she made him get it and bring it up so she could set it up for him.

"You just need a couple of apps," she said as she typed something.

Her phone dinged. "It's from the police again!"

This time the message read:

This is in reference to

Citizen Crime Report: F4927549303

An arrest(s) has been made in this case

Thank you for using the Citizen Crime Reporting Service

"Nice," said Noah.

"Let's celebrate with donuts!" Josh said and climbed down the ladder. Olivia and Noah followed him inside.

"Hi there," said Mom. "You're all up and about pretty early."

"Mom, this is Olivia," Noah introduced them. "We've been working with her on a...project this weekend."

"That's great! Well, Olivia, would you like a donut?" Mom asked. They sat down and ate. The donuts were delicious.

The End

Acknowledgments

I'd like to thank Charley, Naftali, Kiva and Lazar. I'd like to thank my parents and Charley's parents for their love and support along the way. Thank you to my editor Rose Green who helps with all the details.

Thank you to my proofreader Linda Wobus who can solve any mystery.

Thank you to Ms. Jones' 2nd grade class at Roland Park Elementary and to Ms. Jones and Mr. T for giving me class time and encouragement.

Thank you especially to my illustrator Elizabeth Leach for lending her time and talents to a new indie author. Your illustrations are an invaluable part of this project and I couldn't have donut without you!

About the Author

Willow Night lives in a neighborhood in Baltimore with mysterious houses for sale. She checks on them every day.

Find out more at willownight.com.

From The Mystery of the Toxic Playground...

Chapter 1

Noah looked down at his watch. It was time.

"Josh, it's almost three o'clock. I'm going out to the clubhouse now." Noah's younger brother Josh was playing a video game and did not look up.

Josh had been playing this game a lot lately. He used to spend all of his time working on his supplies and making up missions to go on. One of the missions had led the brothers, and their friend Olivia, to discover the truth about a haunted house on Sycamore Street.

But ever since this new game came out, Josh only wanted to play it. All the time. Over and over. Noah liked video games too, but he felt like his little brother never talked to him anymore.

"Hey Josh, Olivia's coming at three. She said she had news," Noah tried again.

"Yeah, one minute," Josh muttered.

Noah rolled his eyes and put on his shoes, heading out the back door to the clubhouse. The boys had built it with Dad a few summers ago. This summer there was a plan to paint the outside.

The sun was bright and hot. Noah climbed up the clubhouse ladder and ducked inside.

There were piles of tools and supplies—Josh's favorite thing to collect.

Dad had helped with waterproofing. There were now windows with screens, which made it harder for Josh to climb in and out the window. But it helped a lot with the bugs.

"Hello? You guys up there?" a voice called from below.

"Hi, Olivia!" A tall girl in jeans and a faded T-shirt was standing her bike up against the fence. She had a ponytail with lots of curly dark hair. Olivia and Noah had both just finished sixth grade.

She turned and grinned, "Hi, Noah. I might have a new case for us to work on. It's pretty interesting." Her grin faded. "But also, pretty serious." Olivia had her messenger bag slung over her shoulder as she climbed up and looked around. "Where's Josh?"

"Don't ask. He's obsessed with a new video game. He says he'll be here in a minute."

"I'll give him one minute." Olivia touched the screen of her smart watch. Noah and Olivia sat in the heat until her watch beeped.

"Okay! I'm going to get him!" Olivia jumped up and left.

She returned right away with Josh. Josh looked grumpy and complained about stopping his game before the end of the level.

"This is more important than a game, Josh," Olivia told him. "We need your help with a new mystery."

Josh still scowled, but he sat down and listened.

"Here's what I know," Olivia started. "Last week I took my little sister Emily to the playground a couple of times. Also last week Emily was sick, feeling bad, and her head hurt."

The boys shrugged. There didn't seem to be a mystery so far unless it was how baby Emily got a cold. Probably by licking something. She did that a lot.

Olivia continued, "Emily wasn't the only kid who got sick after playing at that playground last week. A ton of little kids did."

"Maybe they're picking up germs on the equipment?" Noah asked.

"That's one idea. But they seem to be sick right after they play there, and then they get better the next day. It happened again when I took her on Tuesday."

Josh looked like he was trying to be polite. "Um, Olivia, is this the mystery? Kids getting sick at the playground? Because I have some other stuff I need to do, and I don't even go to that playground anymore."

Noah sighed. That wasn't completely true, because he and Josh still rode down to the playground to fly their drones. They would swing or climb around while they were there. And Noah was pretty sure 'things to do' was just going back to the video game.

Olivia looked annoyed. "Josh, little kids and babies are getting sick at the playground. It means that I don't have a place to take Emily to play, or any of the kids I babysit. It's a pretty big deal for me, and them, and their parents."

"When did this start?" Noah asked.

"I noticed it last week," Olivia explained, "and my mom said that was when she heard other moms talk about their kids coughing and feeling tired after playing there."

"So, what changed last week to make the playground toxic? Wait," Noah thought of something, "did *you* feel sick and tired after going there, Olivia?"

Olivia thought, and she checked a program on her watch. Olivia had a smart watch, and a nice phone, her own computer tablet, and a security system and camera.

Noah and Josh didn't even have phones–Mom and Dad didn't let them–so they tried not to be jealous of Olivia's tech. She did a ton of babysitting to save up the money to pay for it all herself.

"Okay, it looks like I had some minor symptoms. I had lower oxygen when I was at the playground and afterwards for an hour or two," she told them.

"Wow, it knows all that?" Josh asked.

Olivia explained how the watch tracked her heart rate and other vital signs. "It may be more useful than I thought. So should we go down there to see what's up?"

"Sure," Noah said and headed out the door of the clubhouse.

With one last longing look towards the house, and his video game, Josh mumbled okay, and followed.

Made in United States
North Haven, CT
31 October 2023

43449132R00068